To: Dolly

I hope all your
dreams come true.

Under the Angel Tree

The Eileen Series

by Christine Elizabeth Herren

Illustrated by Erin McGuire-Thompson

Under the Angel Tree

By Christine Elizabeth Herren

Illustrated by Erin McGuire-Thompson

Copyright ©2019 by Christine Elizabeth Herren

Illustrations Copyright ©2019 by Erin McGuire-Thompson

Printed On-Demand

Hardcover ISBN 978-1-64338-086-5

24 Hours Books, Inc.

14 S. Queen Street, Mt. Sterling, Kentucky 40353, USA

www.24hourbooks.co

Email orders@24hourbooks.co

Orders 1-800-765-2464

Information 859-520-3757

Text 606-359-2064

Printed and bound in the United States of America

Author's Bio:

Christine Herren's love of children's books began with the collection her mother began for her. A graduate of the University of Kentucky, she studied dance and theatre through high school. An adult collector of children's books, she enjoys discovering new authors and reading again the classics. A writer of poetry and prose, this is her first children's book. She lives in Lexington, Kentucky.

Illustrator's Bio:

Erin McGuire-Thompson creates illustrations for children's books and for editorial use. "Under the Angel Tree" is Erin's first published children's book illustrations and she is currently writing and illustrating several of her own picture books. She is a member of the Society of Children's Book Writers and Illustrators (SCBWI) and the Lexington Art League. She lives in Lexington, KY with her husband and her fur babies. Discover more of her artwork at www.PaisleyToadStudio.com and follow her on Instagram and Facebook.

There was a little girl with red curls named Eileen
who was filled with wonder and imagination.

She liked to dance and twirl to the sounds of music inside her head and spin and chase butterflies.

She loved to pick flowers and chase the rabbits in her grandmother's garden. Butterflies were her best friends and she was happy and content being in her garden.

One day a group of little girls stopped Eileen and asked her why she was always dancing and twirling by herself.

"Riding bicycles is more fun," they said. "You look stupid doing what you are doing" they said. You can ride your bicycle to a friend's house, the movies, or anywhere you want to go." But dancing was what made Eileen happy.

Eileen really didn't know how to ride a bicycle or even like riding a bicycle, but her mother bought her one and tried to teach her how to ride. She wasn't very steady though and this meant she would have a hard time keeping up with the other girls.

One afternoon the girls spotted Eileen trying to ride her bicycle and asked her to go with them on a trail through a park with lots of trees and flowers.

She tried to keep up with them, but when they turned down a different path, she couldn't find them. They were trying to scare her and lose her.

All of a sudden it started to rain. Eileen put her bicycle under the nearest tree and ran and ran until she saw the biggest tree she had ever seen. The branches seemed to reach down and touch her face, protecting her from the pouring rain and wiping away her sadness.

She was so frightened that she began to cry.
Then she looked up at the tree. Suddenly she felt
safe. The tree seemed to be smiling at her and
protecting her.

The rain stopped and Eileen started to dance under the branches of the big tree. She danced and danced under the tree's long branches by herself.

Eileen wasn't sure how long she had been dancing. "Perhaps I should try and find the other girls. I left my bicycle too. I should probably try and find my way back to where I left it."

She hadn't walked very far when she met the group of girls who told her they had been looking for her.

The girls told Eileen they had been watching her dance under the big tree and laughing at how silly she looked by herself. They started to laugh and tell her how funny she looked with her arms waving above her head and her feet skipping around the stump of the big tree.

Eileen only hung her head and tried to act as if their laughter didn't hurt her feelings and make her want to cry. She tried to tell them how she found the tree and how special the tree was and how the tree seemed to smile at her and encourage her to dance.

The girls only laughed more. "Whoever heard of a smiling tree?" They asked. They jumped on their bicycles and rode off down the trail.

Eileen was once again all alone. She wanted to cry, but knew she needed to try and find her bicycle and the path that would lead her home.

She found her way down the trail and saw her bicycle lying under a tree.

She pushed it through the dirt and mud, only to find herself once again standing in front of the big tree.

"Don't be afraid Eileen, a small voice said. Please call me Elizabeth your guardian angel."

"How did you know my name?" asked Eileen. "I know many things, said the voice. I know you are a very special young lady who loves to dance and twirl and chase butterflies in her grandmother 's garden. But you must learn to believe in yourself and trust God. You must know that God gave each of us special gifts."

"But I am different from the other girls. They don't want to play with me or be my friends."

"God put a special light in each of us that he wants to shine, said Elizabeth. You must always remember that."

"Do I have a special light?"

Every time you dance and twirl and be yourself you are letting God's special light shine in you.

The sun began to set and Eileen knew her mother would be worried if she was late getting home.

I will show you the way home, said Elizabeth, don't be afraid."

A beautiful white light suddenly began to shine on the road home for Eileen.

"I don't want to leave you," said Eileen.

"But you are not leaving me. Every time you dance and twirl, every time you let your special light shine, I will be with you. I will be watching you."

She saw a robin sitting on one of the branches and a small rabbit playing under the tree.

Eileen felt very alone. Suddenly she heard Elizabeth's voice once more "Don't be sad. Never forget God made each of us with our own special light. I will always be watching over you from above the branches of our special angel tree."

The End.